The Pain
and
The Great One

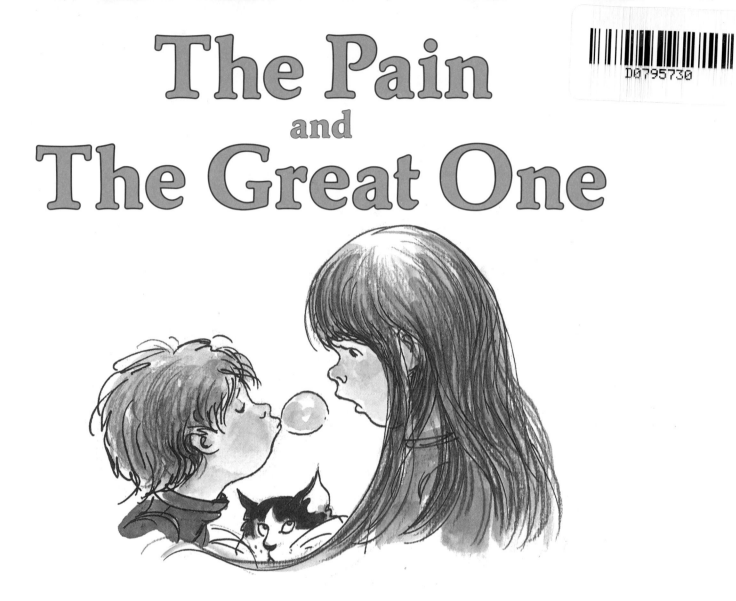

BY JUDY BLUME

Illustrations by Irene Trivas

A PICTURE YEARLING BOOK

To the original Pain and the Great One with Love

Published by
Bantam Doubleday Dell Books for Young Readers
a division of
Bantam Doubleday Dell Publishing Group, Inc.
1540 Broadway
New York, New York 10036

ISBN: 0-440-40967-5

Reprinted by arrangement with Bradbury Press, Inc., an affiliate of Macmillan, Inc.

Printed in the United States of America

September 1985

10   9   8   7

BVG

The Pain

My brother's a pain.
He won't get out of bed
In the morning.
Mom has to carry him
Into the kitchen.
He opens his eyes
When he smells
His corn flakes.

He should get dressed
   himself.
He's six.
He's in first grade.
But he's so pokey
Daddy has to help him
Or he'd never be ready
   in time
And he'd miss the bus.

He cries if I
Leave without him.
Then Mom gets mad
And yells at me
Which is another
    reason why
My brother's a pain.

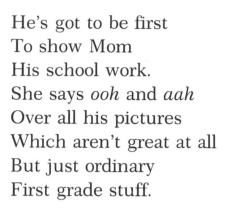

He's got to be first
To show Mom
His school work.
She says *ooh* and *aah*
Over all his pictures
Which aren't great at all
But just ordinary
First grade stuff.

At dinner he picks
At his food.
He's not supposed
To get dessert
If he doesn't
Eat his meat.
But he always
Gets it anyway.

When he takes a bath
My brother the pain
Powders the whole bathroom
And never gets his face clean.
Daddy says
He's learning to
Take care of himself.
I say,
He's a slob!

My brother the pain
Is two years younger than me.
So how come
He gets to stay up
As late as I do?
Which isn't really late enough
For somebody in third grade
Anyway.

I asked Mom and
    Daddy about that.
They said,
"You're right.
You *are* older.
You *should* stay
    up later."

So they tucked the Pain
Into bed.
I couldn't wait
For the fun to begin.
I waited
And waited
And waited.
But Daddy and Mom
Just sat there
Reading books.

Finally I shouted,
"I'm going to bed!"

"We thought you wanted
To stay up later,"
They said.

"I did.
But without the Pain
There's nothing to do!"

"Remember that tomorrow,"
Mom said.
And she smiled.

But the next day
My brother was
     a pain again.
When I got a phone call
He danced all around me
Singing stupid songs
At the top of his lungs.
Why does he have to
     act that way?

And why does he
   always
Want to be
   garbage man
When I build a city
Out of blocks?
Who needs him
Knocking down
   buildings
With his dumb
   old trucks!

And I would really like to know
Why the cat sleeps on the Pain's bed
Instead of mine
Especially since I am the one
Who feeds her.
That is the meanest thing of all!

I don't understand
How Mom can say
The Pain is lovable.
She's always kissing him
And hugging him
And doing disgusting things
Like that.
And Daddy says
The Pain is just what
They always wanted.

YUCK!

I think they love him better than me.

The Great One

My sister thinks she's
   so great
Just because
   she's older
Which makes Daddy
   and Mom think
She's really smart.
But I know the truth.
My sister's a jerk.

She thinks she's great
Just because she can
Play the piano
And you can tell
The songs
    are real ones.
But I like
    my songs better
Even if nobody
Ever heard them before.

My sister thinks she's so great
Just because she can work
The can opener.
Which means she gets
To feed the cat.
Which means the cat
Likes her better than me
Just because she feeds her.

My sister thinks she's so great
Just because Aunt Diana lets
Her watch the baby
And tells her how much
The baby likes *her*.

And all the time
The baby is sleeping
In my dresser drawer.
Which Mom
    has fixed up
Like a bed
For when the baby
Comes to visit.
And I'm not supposed
To touch him
Even if he's
In *my* drawer
And gets changed
On *my* bed.

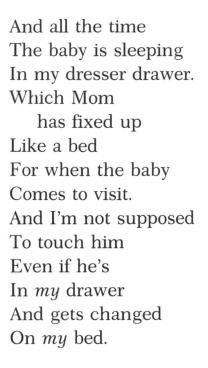

My sister thinks she's so great
Just because she can
Remember phone numbers.
And when she dials
She never gets
The wrong person.

And when she has
    friends over
They build whole cities
Out of blocks.
I like to be garbage man.
I zoom my trucks
    all around.
So what if I
    knock down
Some of their buildings?

"It's not fair
That she always gets
To use
    the blocks!"
I told Daddy
    and Mom.
They said,
"You're right.
Today you can
    use the blocks
All by yourself."

"I'm going to build
    a whole city
Without you!"
I told the Great One.
"Go ahead," she said.
"Go build a whole
    state without me.
See if I care!"

So I did.
I built a whole
    country
All by myself.
Only it's not the
    funnest thing
To play blocks alone.

Because when I
    zoomed my trucks
And knocked down
    buildings
Nobody cared but me!

"Remember that tomorrow,"
Mom said, when I told her
I was through playing blocks.

But the next day
We went swimming.
I can't stand my sister
When we go swimming.
She thinks she's so great
Just because she can
    swim and dive
And isn't afraid
To put her face
In the water.
I'm scared to
    put mine in
So she calls me *baby*.

Which is why
I have to
Spit water at her
And pull her hair
And even pinch her
        sometimes.

And I don't think it's fair
For Daddy and Mom to yell at me
Because none of it's my fault.
But they yell anyway.

Then Mom hugs my sister
And messes with her hair
And does other disgusting things
Like that.
And Daddy says
The Great One is just what
They always wanted.

YUCK!

I think they love her better than me.